For Hannah, Bridget and Sam – B.M.

Text copyright © Barbara Mitchelhill 1999
Illustrations copyright © Peter Dennis 1999

First published in 1999
by Macdonald Young Books

This edition published in 2009 by Wayland

The right of Barbara Mitchelhill to be identified as the author
and Peter Dennis the illustrator of this Work has been
asserted by them in accordance with the
Copyright, Designs and Patents Act 1988.

A catalogue record for this book is available from
the British Library.

ISBN: 978 0 7502 5749 7

Printed in China

Wayland
338 Euston Road, London NW1 3BH

Wayland is a division of Hachette Children's Books,
an Hachette UK Company
www.hachette.co.uk

The Root of Evil

Barbara Mitchelhill

Illustrated by Peter Dennis

WAYLAND

Chapter One

If they hadn't found the pocket watch, it would never have happened. But that was how it began on the last day of their holiday.

They had been climbing an old stone wall when Jake slipped and fell. As some of the stones broke away, they saw the pocket watch among the dust and the rubble. Its gold casing glinted in the sun.

"Look what fell out of the wall!" called Wez and he clambered over the stones towards it.

Jake was sitting on the ground, rubbing his knee. "What about me?" he groaned. "My leg's broken. Give me a hand, will you."

"Your leg's not broken," said Amy. "Get up and stop moaning."

Wez picked up the watch and blew the dust off the face. He could see it was very old. Very special.

"Amazing!" he said. "I've never seen a watch like it."

Jake was sulking. "Call that a watch?" he said, struggling to his feet. "Now *this* is a watch!"

He held out his wrist. He was wearing a stainless-steel chronograph watch with a date display, calendar and twelve-hour stopwatch. He had saved for a year to buy it.

It was awesome. "*This* is what you call a watch," he repeated.

But they were not listening. They were staring at the gold pocket watch. "There's something on the back," said Wez and rubbed it on his T-shirt to remove the dust.

Carved into the gold plate were the letters Z G and the date 1860. "It must be worth a fortune. We'd better take it to the police station."

Jake reached out and snatched it from Wez. "No way!" he said. "We'll sell it and blow the money on the fun-fair."

"You can't!" yelled Wez. "That's stealing!"

"Who'll know about it?" said Amy. "It's been here for years."

"Yeah!" said Jake. "I found it, didn't I? Well... finders keepers!"

Wez felt a cold chill ripple down his spine. As he saw Jake clutch the pocket watch, he knew something bad was going to happen.

Chapter Two

"So how are you going to sell it?" Amy asked. "Hold an auction?"

"No, dummy! Go to an antique shop in Bidmouth. They'll give us a good price."

There was a street in Bidmouth called Abbott's Way. It was narrow and cobbled and ran up the side of the hill that bordered the town. It was lined with small shops. Tea rooms. Second hand book shops. Junk shops.

It was there that they found Abbott's Way Antiques.

"Right!" said Jake. "Let's go in."

They pushed open the door and a rusty bell echoed inside. They stepped into a room which was small and crammed with old furniture. Cobwebs hung from low rafters and a film of dust covered everything. The room was so dark that they didn't notice something in the corner, a thin, hunched figure dressed in black.

"Can I help you?" croaked a voice. They jumped nervously.

"Are… are you the shopkeeper?" asked Jake.

"I am."

The dark shape shuffled nearer.

"We want to sell this watch," said Jake. "How much—"

"Ah!" interrupted the shopkeeper. "But is it *yours* to sell?"

Amy blushed and gripped Wez's hand.

"It was my grandad's," Jake lied and put it on the counter. "He left it to me when he died."

The shopkeeper's hand, which was cracked and paper dry, reached out and took the watch. For a while, no one spoke. No one moved. Then, without a word, the old man opened a drawer, took out some notes and dropped them on the counter.

"Five hundred pounds," he said.

They were stunned. They hadn't expected so much.

Jake swallowed hard. "OK. Thanks."
He reached over, picked up the money and
turned to go.

But before they reached the door, the
shopkeeper spoke again. "But if you change
your mind, return the money. Keep it and
regret it. I'll be waiting."

Chapter Three

"Five hundred pounds!" shrieked Amy. "We're rich!"

Only Wez was unhappy. "The watch wasn't ours. That money belongs to somebody else."

The others ignored him.

"Come on!" said Jake. "Just think what we can do with the money."

"Yeah! How about buying that for starters?" said Amy, pointing across the street to a junk shop. A red bike stood outside with a notice on it which said 'One owner. Cheap for a quick sale.'

"You can't buy a bike!" said Wez. "What will you tell your dad?"

Jake laughed. "I'll just say somebody gave it to me."

He disappeared into the shop and, when he came out, he was followed by a tall man in a brown overall.

"Mind how you go, son," he said. Then he released the safety lock on the bike and handed it to Jake.

Jake was grinning from ear to ear. "Isn't she a beauty?" he said, flinging his leg over the bike. "I bet she'll go like the wind."

"Hey!" said Amy. "I want a go, too! Let me ride piggy."

She grabbed hold of Jake's shoulders and heaved herself up behind him. She sat on the saddle, her legs dangling while Jake's feet began to push on the peddles.

"See you at the bottom of the hill, Wez!" they yelled, laughing hysterically.

Wez watched them set off and suddenly he felt scared. He wanted them to stop.

They called again. "See ya, Wez!" as they rode away.

The wheels spun round. Faster. Faster. Faster. They were heading down the hill, towards the High Street at the bottom. There was traffic. Cars. Buses. Lorries.

"Jake!" screamed Amy. "Slow down! Stop, will you? *Stop*!"

"I'm trying!" he yelled. "I'm squeezing the brakes. But they won't work!"

Chapter Four

They had no choice.

"We'll have to jump!" yelled Amy. "*Now!*"

They took a deep breath and leaped off the bike. They spun through the air, then *crash*! They landed on the pavement, the wind knocked out of them. They lay there gasping. Their eyes were fixed on the red bike still tearing headlong down the hill.

"No!" screamed Amy, as it ploughed into the High Street. In seconds, the metal frame smashed against a car. It was tossed in the air, then mangled beneath the wheels of a juggernaut. Splintered. Shredded.

"You must be mad," yelled Wez racing towards them. "You could have been killed."

Jake nodded and struggled to his feet. "Come on. We'll have to run for it!" he said. "If they find out that's our bike, we'll be in trouble!"

They raced up Abbott's Way and turned down one of the side streets.

"It wasn't my fault," said Jake, pausing to get his breath. "The brakes were no good."

Amy shrugged. "Forget it. We've still got loads of money. Let's go to the fairground."

"Excellent!" laughed Jake. "We'll go on all the rides. We'll have a great time!"

But Jake was wrong – very wrong indeed.

Chapter Five

The fairground was on the edge of the town. It came every summer for two weeks. There were computer games and dodgems, a ghost train and a big dipper.

"Let's try the Laser Warriors game," said Amy. "It's supposed to be awesome!"

"Maybe later," said Jake. "We'll try that one first." He was pointing to an old-fashioned machine in the corner. On top was a glass case with a dummy's head in it.

"That's gruesome," said Wez. "What does it do?"

"Can't you read?" mocked Jake. "You put your hand in that hole, then the dummy tells your fortune."

Amy laughed. "Let me have a go."

"Me first!" said Jake and fed some money into the slot.

There was a whirring and clunking as the dummy's mouth opened – it began to speak.

"Put your hand in the slot. Slowly."

The voice was deep and dark and evil. It made Jake shiver.

"What are you waiting for?" said Amy. "Are you chicken, or what? Go on! Do it!"

Slowly, he pushed his hand into the hole. He didn't know why, but his heart was pounding wildly and sweat had broken out on his forehead.

Suddenly, the dummy in the case turned its head and looked straight at him. It was terrifying. Jake felt trapped like a rabbit in the headlights of a car. He couldn't move. Then, something inside the hole clamped his hand tight. He felt pain shoot through his wrist. He wanted to scream. He opened his mouth.

No sound came – except the voice of the dummy. "*Keep it and regret it!*" it said. "*Keep it and regret it!*"

Jake felt sick. His head began to spin. Then everything went black.

Chapter Six

"Get up Jake!" laughed Amy. "Stop fooling around!"

"I'm not!" said Jake, rubbing his swollen wrist. "That hurt!"

"No big deal!" said Amy. "It was only a joke."

Wez shook his head. "I don't think it was."

"Oh, lighten up, you two! You're boring. Let's go on the ghost train."

Amy ran over to the pay desk and the boys followed her. They climbed into one of the cars and – before they could catch their breath – the train moved forward. Double doors opened and they entered a weird tunnel lit with dim red lights.

"Spooky!" said Wez.

The train whipped along, flinging them to the side of the car. They laughed as it whizzed round bends. They screamed as a ghost leaped through the wall and skeletons dropped from the ceiling. Lights flashed. Chains clanked. There were screams, shouts and groans. The noise was deafening.

Then the train stopped.

Silence.

They waited but nothing happened.

"Why doesn't somebody do something?" said Jake.

Wez stood up. "H-have you noticed? There's nobody else on the train!"

The others looked over their shoulders. It was true. All the other cars were empty.

They shouted for help but no one heard them. Their voices were swallowed up by the tunnels. They were alone in the long twisting passages. Nothing could be worse.

Then the dim red lights went out.

They clung together in the dark, terrified.

"C-couldn't we walk down the track?" said Amy.

Jake shook his head. "No way!" he said. "It's electrified. As soon as they switch the current back on, we'd be fried!"

Wez leaned out of the car and felt along the side.

"There's a narrow ledge next to the track. If we're careful, we could make it along there."

They were trembling with fear. But they
had to try. With Jake in the lead, they got
out of the car. They shuffled slowly, step by
step, along the ledge, clinging on to the sides
of the tunnel.

Suddenly, Jake screamed. "Aaaagggh!"
The wall had caved in and he fell through it.

"Help!" he yelled.

There was a splash. Jake was plunged into
icy water. He thrashed about, gasping for air.
He tried to grab hold of something.
Anything. But there was nothing.

And he began to sink.

Chapter Seven

Jake didn't give up. He pushed hard on the bottom of the pool and shot back to the surface. Somehow, Amy and Wez managed to grab his hands.

"We've got you!" yelled Wez. "Pull, Amy, pull!"

They dragged him out, choking and gasping for air. He was safe. But not for long.

As Jake struggled to his feet, a white mist rolled down the tunnel. It moved quickly. Surrounding them. Biting cold like a winter frost. And they began to shake.

Then, through the mist, came a glowing shape. Small at first but growing bigger. A spectre was moving towards them.

"What is it?" said Amy.

"What's it saying?"

At first, they couldn't hear. Then, as the spectre came nearer, they knew.

"*Keep it and regret it!*" Those words again.

Their pulses raced. Their hearts beat fiercely.

Wez had understood from the beginning. Now the others knew what was happening, and they were terrified.

"It's the watch," said Amy, her voice shaking. "We shouldn't have sold it. When we spend the money something awful happens. First the bike. Then the fun-fair."

Jake could hardly speak. He was rigid with terror. The spectre was getting closer. Closer.

"W-what can we do?" he stammered.

"Take the money back and get the watch," said Wez. "Find its real owner. Give it back."

"But what about the spectre and the mist!" said Amy. "I'm scared!"

"Run through it!" said Wez. "We've got to."

It was their only chance to escape. They put their heads down and *ran*.

Chapter Eight

They raced down the tunnel. Past the phantom. Through the choking mist. On until they burst through a door and into the blinding daylight.

Even then they didn't stop. They bolted through the fairground, pushing through the crowds and out of the gate. On along the road, down the High Street until their lungs were bursting.

"Nearly there," gasped Wez and they turned up the hill to Abbott's Way.

At the top, they stopped and leaned against the wall, gasping for air and trying to slow their racing hearts.

Abbott's Way Antiques was only a few metres away. The door was open as if they were expected.

"Let's go," said Jake at last. "Let's get rid of the money before it's too late."

They pushed open the door of the shop and stepped into the small room. In the shadows, was the thin, hunched figure standing behind the counter.

"You've come back," he croaked. "How can I help you?"

They inched nervously towards him. Jake in the lead.

"You said I could return the money if I wanted," he said, reaching into his pocket.

"Yes," said the shopkeeper. "Five hundred pounds."

Suddenly Jake realized. He didn't have five hundred pounds! They had spent some of it. They had bought the bike and paid for the fun-fair.

"I-I've got four hundred."

"But you want the gold pocket watch?"

"Yes," said Jake.

"I need five hundred pounds."

In desperation, Jake looked down at his wrist and unfastened his stainless-steel chronograph watch. "Will you take this to make up the missing money?"

"No!" said Amy, rushing forward. "You can't! You saved up all year for that!"

Jake looked at her and shrugged. Then he placed his watch on the counter.

The old man scooped it into his bony hand and dropped it into a drawer. Then he counted the notes Jake had put in front of him and nodded with satisfaction.

"The pocket watch," said Jake. "Can I have it back?"

The shopkeeper look at him sharply. "Haven't you learned your lesson? The watch wasn't yours."

Wez stepped forward. "We want to take it to the police. They'll find the owner."

The old man smiled and his paper thin skin creased into a thousand cracks.

"My name is Zebidiah Gressling. You have *found* the owner."

The kids stared, not believing what he said. Then they turned and fled. They raced down the street, flying over the pavement, stumbling and gasping.

As they stopped for breath, they looked over their shoulders. But they saw nothing familiar. Abbott's Way and the antique shop had disappeared from sight.

DARE TO BE SCARED!

Are you brave enough to try more titles in the Tremors series? They're guaranteed to chill your spine...

Play... if you dare by Ruth Symes

Josie can hardly believe her luck when she finds the computer game at a car boot sale. "Play... if you dare," the game challenges. So she does. Further and further she plays, each level of the game scarier than the last. Then she reaches the last level. "Play... if you dare," repeats the game. But if she does, she could be trapped for ever...

The Claygate Hound by Jan Dean

On the school camp to Claygate, Billy is determined to scare everyone with his terrifying stories of the Claygate Hound, a vicious ghost dog said to lurk nearby. Ryan and Zeb ignore his warnings and explore the woods. They hear a ghostly howl – and run. Has Billy been speaking the truth, or is there a more terrifying reason for what they have heard?

The Curse of the Frozen Loch by Anthony Masters

Why does the ghostly figure skate the loch in the dead of night? And what is wrong with Great-Aunt Fiona? Will and Sarah are determined to solve the mystery and save Fiona. But will they be the next victims of the curse of the frozen loch?

The Ghosts of Golfhawk School by Tessa Potter

Martin and Dan love frightening the younger children at school with scary ghost stories. But then Kirsty arrives. Kirsty claims that she can actually see ghosts. Then a mysterious virus sweeps through the school. Martin is still sure she is lying. After all – ghosts don't exist, do they?

All these books and many more can be purchased from your local bookseller. For more information about Tremors, write to: The Sales Department, Hachette Children's Books, 338 Euston Road, London NW1 3BH.